**Open the door,
and what do you see?**

BEAR AT HOME

Written by Stella Blackstone
Illustrated by Debbie Harter

This is bear's house,
and this is the key.

This is the kitchen,
all clean and neat,

And this is the dining room, where bear likes to eat.

This is the playroom,
with a great big toy chest,

And this is the sitting room,
where bear likes to rest.

This is the hallway,
where bear climbs the stairs,

And this is the library, with big, cosy chairs.

This is the bathroom,
with walls painted bright,

And this is the bedroom, where bear says goodnight!

GROUND FLOOR

Playroom

Dining room

Kitchen

Sitting room

Hallway

FIRST FLOOR

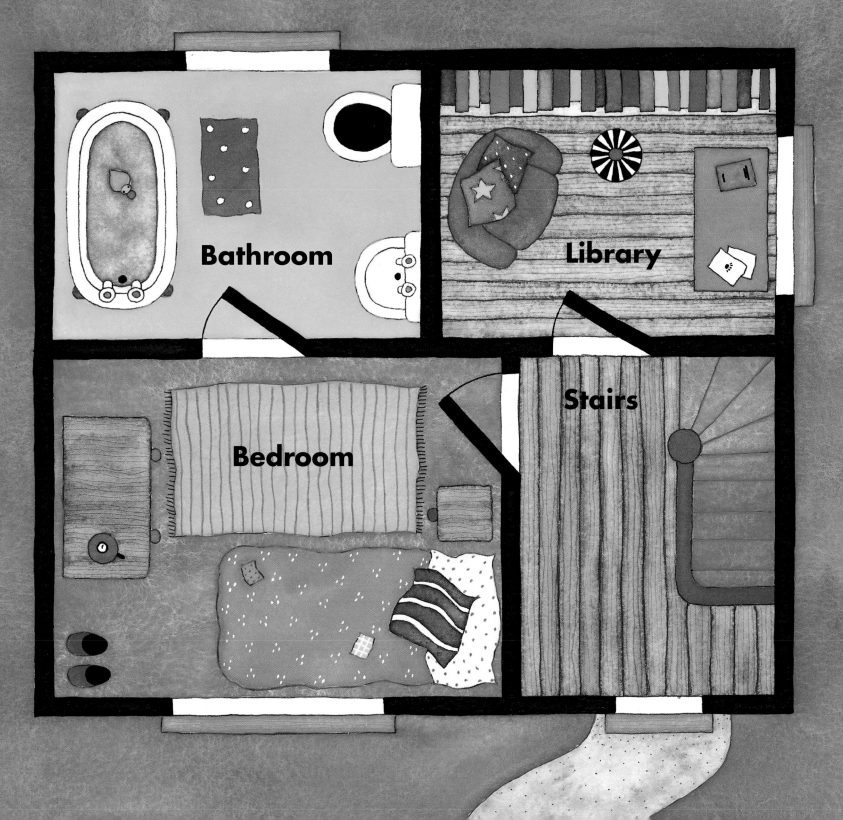

Bathroom

Library

Bedroom

Stairs

To Bryony and Sarah — D. H.
To Benedict — S. B.

Barefoot Books
124 Walcot Street
Bath
BA1 5BG

First published in Great Britain in 2001 by Barefoot Books Ltd

This book was typeset in Futura
The illustrations were prepared in watercolour,
pen and ink and crayon on thick watercolour paper

Graphic design by Polka. Creation, Bath
Colour separation by Grafiscan, Verona
Printed and bound in Singapore by Tien Wah Press Pte Ltd

This book has been printed on 100% acid-free paper

Hardcover ISBN 1 84148-434-2
Paperback ISBN 1 84148-435-0

British Cataloguing-in-Publication Data: a catalogue record
for this book is available from the British Library

3 5 7 9 8 6 4 2